For Miss Essie who loved New Orleans.
—R.W.G.

Thanks to friends and family worldwide.
—D.W.

Special book excerpts or customized printings can also be created to fit specific needs. For details, write or call the Marimba Books special sales department:

MARIMBA BOOKS, P.O. Box 5306
East Orange, NJ 07019, 973.672.7701

MARIMBA BOOKS and the Marimba Books logo are trademarks of The Hudson Publishing Group L.L.C.
Distributed by Just Us Books, Inc.
JustUsBooks.com

Text and cover design by Stephan Hudson

ISBN-13: 978-1-60349-030-6
ISBN: 10 1-60349-031-0
e-ISBN: 978-1-933491-92-9

First Marimba Books printing 2015
10 9 8 7 6 5 4 3 2 1

Printed in the United States of America

An imprint of The Hudson Publishing Group L.L.C.

Bottle Cap Boys
Dancing on Royal Street

By Rita Williams-Garcia
Illustrated by Damian Ward

Two boys meet on Royal Street.

Rudy on one side,

Randy on the other.

Two boys meet on Royal Street
to see

"Who dances best?"

"Me or my brother?"

"Bottle cap

-SLAM-

on my right shoe."

"Bottle cap

-BAM-

on my left shoe."

Tip boxes down
On the ground means
Rudy and Randy are ready to jam!

"Brother, I'll show you how to do it."

CLICKITY, CLACK, CLACK

CLICKITY, CLACK, CLACK

Folks start
to gather
Folks crowd
around.

Folks stop
to watch
Two brothers
get down.

"Say mister, mister!
Throw me a dollar, holler
Mister, mister, a quarter or a dime."

"Hey, mister, mister!
Throw me a dollar.
'Cause who dances best
Eats good tonight."

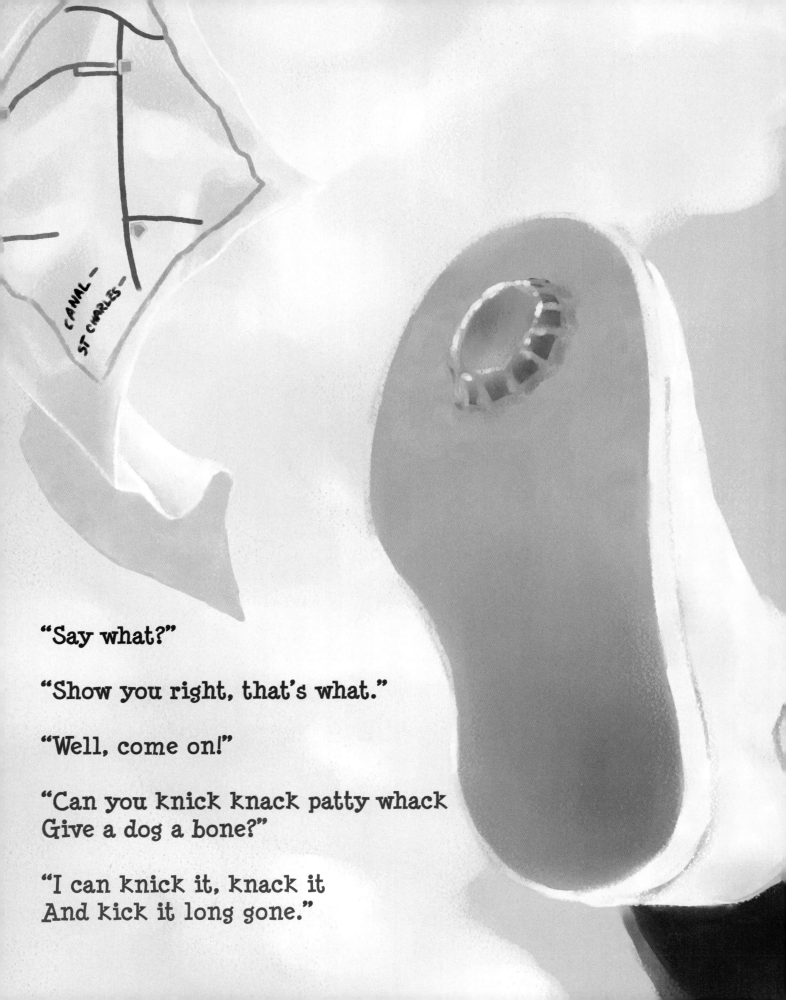

"Say what?"

"Show you right, that's what."

"Well, come on!"

"Can you knick knack patty whack
Give a dog a bone?"

"I can knick it, knack it
And kick it long gone."

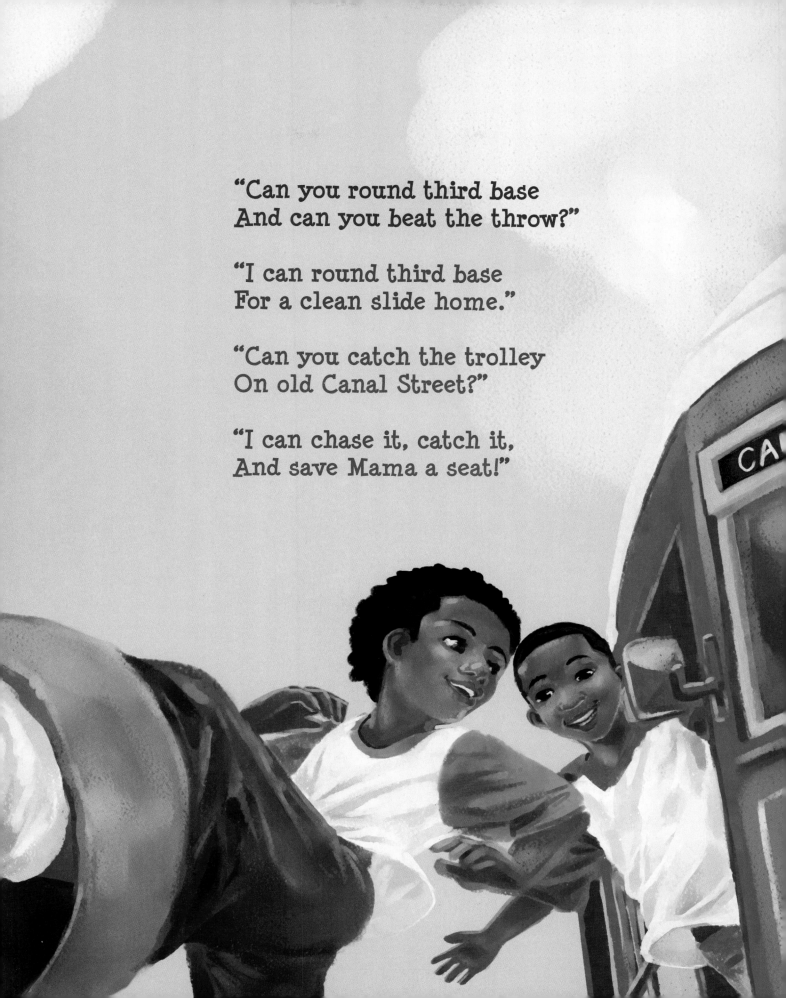

"Can you round third base
And can you beat the throw?"

"I can round third base
For a clean slide home."

"Can you catch the trolley
On old Canal Street?"

"I can chase it, catch it,
And save Mama a seat!"

"Well, look out!
Coins raining in my tip box
Copper and silver falling out the sky."

"Look out!
Coins raining in my tip box
Just don't let my dollar bills fly."

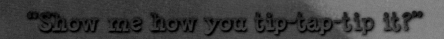

CLICKITY, CLACK, CLACK
CLICKITY, CLACK, CLACK

"Show me how you tip-tap-tip it?"

TIPITY-TAP, TAP TAP
TIPITY-TAP, TAP TAP

"If you show me how you click-clack-click it."

Let's
CLICK!/ TIP!/ CLACK!

All together with a
TIPITY!/ CLICKITY!/ TIP!/

Mix it up with some
CLICK-IT!/ TIP-IT!/ TAP-IT!/

Bottle caps gotta
SLIP-IT/ HIT-IT SLAP IT
Well, all right!

Keep the good times rolling
And the silver coins flowing!

"Can you taste it, brother?
Can you taste your dreams?"

"Can you taste it, brother?
Close your eyes and see."

Pralines and beignets, soft and sweet
Jambalaya and red beans to jump for joy

A hot Lucky Dog, now that's a treat
And po'boys for poor boys,
We can't be beat!

Two boys jammed on Royal Street

Rudy on one side,

Randy on the other.

Two boys jammed on Royal Street.

"I'm a bottle cap king!"

"And so is my brother."

Dear Reader,

When I visited the city of New Orleans in the 1990s I fell in love with its lively music and traditional Creole and Cajun dishes. The unique townhouses and occasional horse-driven carriages gave the city a storybook look. Everywhere I turned, street performers entertained visitors and locals. I always carried a few dollar bills and coins to drop inside tip boxes.

While the city of New Orleans is rich in culture, ethnic diversity, and history, New Orleans is also economically among the poorest cities in the United States. Still, the people of New Orleans remain resourceful. By combining culture and talents, the people of New Orleans find ways to turn adversity into commerce while treating spectators to a taste of the city's rich heritage.

The central square known as the "French Quarter," hosts a variety of street performers, from seasoned musicians, to young bottle cap dancers. Bottle cap dancers stamp and grind bottle caps into the bottom soles of their sneakers, until the bottle caps stay firmly in place at the toe. Armed with a cardboard box for tips, a lot of charm, and energy, these young tappers dance hard for their tips. Bottle cap dancers dance with the same energy for small crowds, as they would for one spectator. The most popular bottle cap dancers are as young as four years old, and as old as teenagers. In a craft where "cute" is king, the younger dancers can earn more tips than older performers. The money dropped into tip boxes helps to support the dancers' struggling families. Often, a parent or older sibling watches nearby to protect the younger dancers from thieves.

Before there were bottle cap dancers and tap dancers, there were the syncopated hand clapping, foot stomping and traditions of African dance called, "Juba" and European jigs and clogging styles. The influences of Africans and Europeans of the 19th century evolved into tap dance, an American dance form. In rural Fitzgerald, Georgia, young Charles "Chuck" Green put bottle caps on his bare feet and danced on streets for onlookers. Dancing with bottle caps soon caught on among talented but hungry children in New Orleans and is still going strong.

Years ago, I watched with the nation as Hurricane Katrina, a powerful category 5 hurricane, devastated New Orleans. Raging Hurricane Katrina washed away homes, businesses, landmarks, and lives. Among the hardest hit were the poor, the aged, and the children.

I have since visited New Orleans several times. With help from both wealthy and impoverished nations around the world, the "Crescent City" continues to rebuild the hopes of its people. This rich culture and its people cannot be washed away. It is a privilege to pay tribute to the city and its youngest artists.

Sincerely,

Rita Williams-Garcia

Reader Tip Box

References mentioned or illustrated in
Bottle Cap Boys Dancing on Royal Street:

Beignet [ben-yay] a deep-fried pastry brought over to Louisiana by French immigrants in the 18th century. This breakfast food is dipped in powdered sugar and served with New Orleans coffee at Café Du Monde and other shops in the French Quarter.

The French Quarter, the oldest neighborhood in New Orleans, dates back to the 1700s. This central square and marketplace now features a variety of art, street performances, local food, and the unique architecture of New Orleans.

Jambalaya is a Louisiana chicken and rice dish with roots in French and Spanish cuisine. The key ingredients are rice, chicken, andouille [an-doo-wee] sausage, seafood and Creole spices.

King Cake is an oval ringed cinnamon roll cake, decorated with white icing, and Mardi Gras colors of gold, green and purple, which stand for power, justice and faith. The person who finds the tiny plastic baby Jesus placed in the cake, is crowned "King for a Day." The king cake is served 12 days after Christmas, or on "Twelfth Night," and ends on Fat Tuesday, or Mardi Gras.

*Lucky Dogs® are hot dogs sold from a hot dog shaped cart, complete with bun and wiener. Lucky Dogs are popular in the French Quarter and are enjoyed by street performers and tourists, alike.

A **Po'Boy** is a sandwich served on French bread, traditionally with bits of roast beef drowned in gravy. This sandwich is said to date back to the streetcar workers strike during The Great Depression. Today the sandwich is made in a number of varieties, including shrimp, oyster, catfish, or sausage, and topped with pickles, lettuce, tomato and mayonnaise.

Pralines are round disk-shaped candies made of brown sugar, white sugar, cream, butter and pecans. The treat dates back to the 1700s. After the Emancipation, newly freed black women earned a living by cooking and then selling pralines in the French Quarter.

Red Beans and Rice is a red kidney beans and rice dish combined with bits of ham for a smoky flavor. Red beans and rice is traditionally served on Mondays.

Royal Street features antique shops, art galleries, fine dining, and townhouses with iron lace balconies–offering an elegant contrast to raucous Bourbon Street. Royal Street is also a favorite spot for bottle cap dancers hoping to attract patrons.

The oldest passenger **streetcar** in the United States can be found in New Orleans. The St. Charles Avenue Line streetcar dates back to 1835 and still runs today. The curve of the St. Charles Avenue Line, together with the Canal Street Line, resemble the shape of a baseball diamond.

Spectators drop dollar bills and coins into tip boxes to show street performers their appreciation. The cardboard flaps of the **tip box** help to keep dollar bills from being carried away by a strong wind.

*Lucky Dog® is a registered trademark of Lucky Dog, Inc.